GET HAPPY!

40 ways to beat the blues.

A book to pick up when you are feeling low. Forty ideas for triggering happiness!

GET HAPPY!

40 ways to beat the blues.

by
Helen D. Wright, Ph.D.

Illustrated by Alice Black

PRICE/STERN/SLOAN
Publishers, Inc., Los Angeles
1983

Formerly printed under the title *"Relief from Depression."*

Copyright© 1978 by Helen D. Wright, Ph. D.
Published by Price/Stern/Sloan Publishers, Inc.
410 North La Cienega Boulevard, Los Angeles, California 90048

ISBN: 0-8431-0430-9

DEDICATED TO

Anyone who wishes to make his or her
world, or "our" world, a more
joyful place.

CONTENTS

FOREWORD

When depression strikes, precious hours, energy, money and relationships may be wasted. With that low feeling comes a constriction in the thinking processes that tend to inhibit the flow of beneficial ideas and effective solutions.

This idea book has been created specifically for the purpose of priming and stimulating the thinking processes so that a person may trigger the latch on the trap of simple depression and free himself or herself to live happily again.

These suggestions were collected from the personal experiences of the author and her patients. Dr. Wright has worked in the mental health field for over seventeen years.

In cases of severe or prolonged depression, by all means, consult professional help.

Many persons have reported higher mood states from just browsing through the book.

Try it!

Three Preliminary Steps

1   Label the feeling: "I am depressed*"
Further clarify your mood by recognizing:

"I feel…(select one)

…helpless	…angry
…hopeless	…anxious
…a loss	…worthless
…numb	…guilty."

2   Recognize and affirm strongly:
"I am in charge of my life. I will use my
own power and do what it takes to find
my way out of this."

3   Be sure you are not simply overtired.
If you are, try to get some rest.

*Depression is defined here as the feeling of being "stuck,"
dejected, immobilized or too miserable to function well.

The
40
suggestions

Choose and do one or several
of the following activities.
Pay close attention to your mood changes
so that you may learn what
triggers higher mood states for you.

Think of something you want that
is available; then make a plan
to get it.

Go for a long walk.

Think of people who bring you up; call one of them.

Listen to your favorite music.

Sing or chant.

Do something creative.

Take a shower or a long, warm bath.

Make a list of your strengths.
Spend at least an hour concentrating
fully on appreciating yourself.

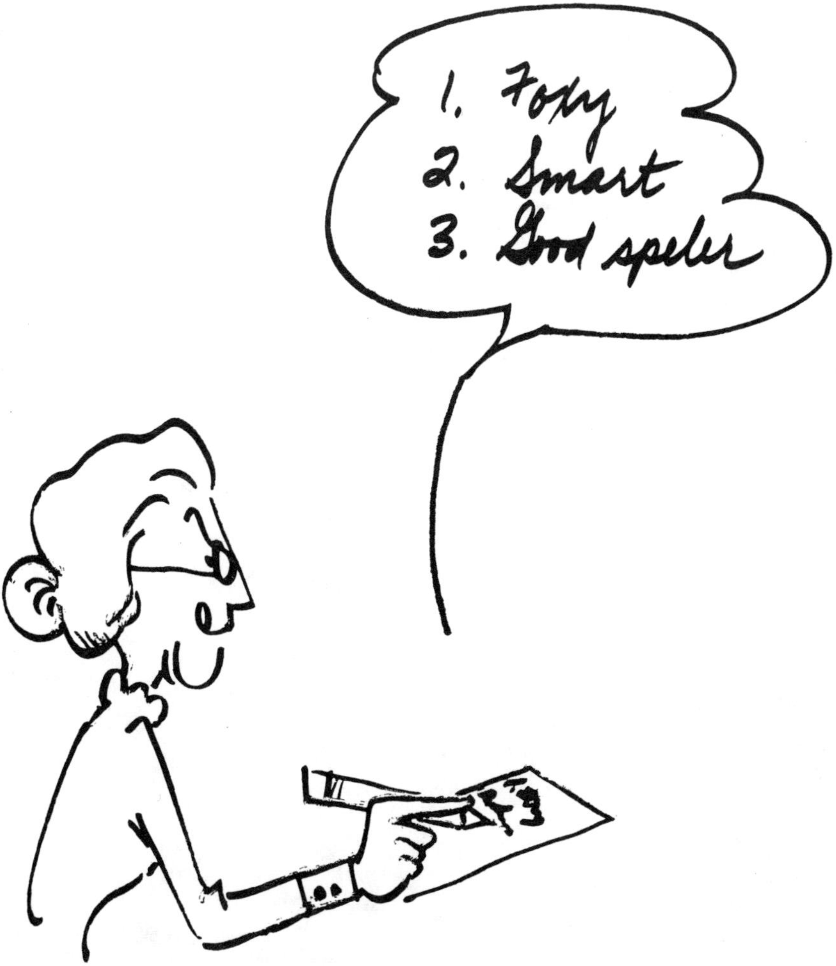
1. Foxy
2. Smart
3. Good speler

Love a pet expressively.

**If you have suffered a loss,
get started on a plan
to find something even better!**

Dance!

Forgive someone.

**Consult a nutrition book
and consider
what you might add to your diet
for pep and vitality.**

Plan a trip or event
that you think you would enjoy.
Spend an hour anticipating
in fantasy exciting aspects
of the experience.

**Think about enjoyable ways
of relaxing;
choose one and do it.**

Make an appointment for a massage, or give yourself a body massage or an invigorating skin brush.

Exercise.

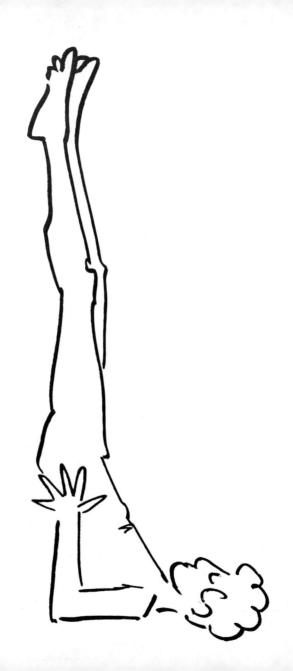

**Begin something
you have been putting off
for a long time.**

Dear Aunt Sophie,
Thanks for the great sweater you sent me for my 19th birthday...

Start your own humor book.
Write down the funniest jokes
you can remember.

Relive the "greatest moment"
you ever had.

**Stop doing anything
and just BE for awhile.**

**Try to think
of a specific solution to
the biggest problem in your life.**

**Make a list
of things you are grateful for.**

Scream!

Think of a goal
that will bring you joy.
Then consider ways to attain it.

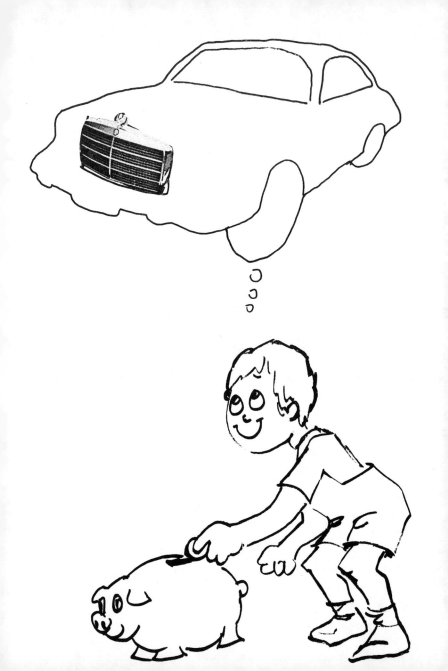

Resolve to free yourself
from the fear and anger in your life.
Start by realizing you can't
blame other people or things
for your problems.

Much unhappiness
is caused by lack of knowledge.
Learn how to get what you want
by looking for the missing information,
the right teacher or
a satisfying philosophy of life.

**Arrange a meeting
with your favorite person.**

Give something away.

Tell someone you love him/her.

Make a list
of things you feel guilty about.
Consider where you can make amends.
Make amends.
Burn the list.

Plan a surprise for someone.

Clean up something.

**Anticipate the pleasure
of eating your favorite meal.**

Organize a part of your life
that has been producing irritation.

**Relive
with vivid imagination
an experience in your life
which made you feel extremely loved.**

Check to see if your life
is out of balance
in regard to work and play,
rest and activity,
excitement and calm.
If you decide it is,
make a plan to restore the balance.

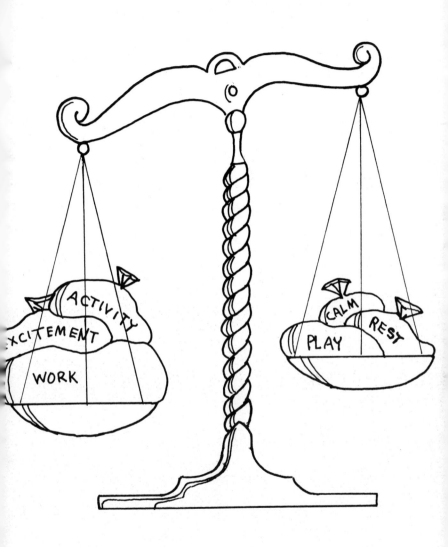

Relax beside a cozy fire.

Listen to the wisdom in silence.

**Make a map
of your own way out of depression.
Watch the changes in yourself
and make a record of what
"brings you up."**

_____

_____

_____

_____

_____

_____

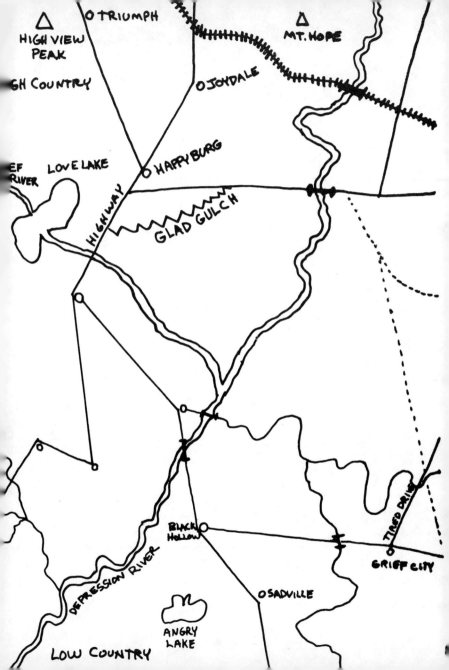

MY FAVORITE IDEAS FROM THE BOOK

_____

_____

_____

_____

_____

_____

_____

_____

This book is published by

PRICE/STERN/SLOAN

Publishers, Inc., Los Angeles

publishers of

I WANT TO CHANGE BUT I DON'T KNOW HOW ($5.95)

FROM HERE TO GREATER HAPPINESS ($3.95)

YOU CAN REWRITE YOUR LIFE ($5.95)

WORLD'S WORST JOKES ($1.75)

FUNNIEST RIDDLES OF THE CENTURY ($1.75)

**MURPHY'S LAW AND OTHER REASONS
WHY THINGS GO ƆNOɹW! ($2.95)**

**MURPHY'S LAW/BOOK TWO and
BOOK THREE ($2.95 each)**

and many, many more

They are available wherever books are sold, or may be ordered directly from the publisher by sending check or money order for the total amount of each book plus $1.00 for handling and mailing. For a complete list of titles send a *stamped, self-addressed envelope* to:

PRICE/STERN/SLOAN *Publishers, Inc.*
410 North La Cienega Boulevard, Los Angeles, California 90048